To CHARLENE! ♥ LOVE, JANE

Ping Meets Pang

A story of otherness, differences, and friendship

Written and illustrated by
Mary Jane Begin

Wyatt-MacKenzie Publishing
DEADWOOD, OREGON

Dedication

To my brother Craig,
to my nephew Craig.

Soaring on wings,
forever in my heart.

Hardcover ISBN: 9781948018876
Softcover ISBN: 9781954332089
eBook ISBN: 9781954332096
Library of Congress Control Number: 2021936465

Wyatt-MacKenzie Publishing
DEADWOOD, OREGON

Welcome to Panda Palace!

Ping, a red panda, lived on
one side of Panda Palace
with other red pandas.

Pang, a giant panda, lived on the other side of Panda Palace with giant pandas.

Ping was proud
to be a panda!

Pang was proud
to be a panda!

Ping liked to poke around,
and find secret hiding places
in Panda Palace.

Pang liked to take naps,
hiding in places no one
else could find.

"What are you?" asked Ping,
surprising a sleepy
Pang.

"I'm Pang. I'm a panda! What are you?"

"I'm Ping. *I'm* a panda!"

"No way!" said Pang. "Pandas are black and white, like me."

"No, they're not!" said Ping. "Pandas are black and red, like me."

"Pandas have pointy ears," said Ping.

"Pandas have round ears,"
said Pang.

"PANDAS have little round tails," said Pang.

"PANDAS
have long
fluffy tails,"
said Ping.

"PANDAS like
to sleep…"
yawned Pang.

"PANDAS like to climb trees!" declared Ping.

"PANDAS are BIG!" shouted Pang.

"PANDAS are SMALL!" shouted Ping.

"PANDAS LOVE BAMBOO!"
hooted Ping.

"PANDAS LOVE BAMBOO!"
hollered Pang.

The pandas stared at each other
for a very long time.

"How could it be?" they both wondered.
"We're different **AND** we're the same."

"You **ARE** a panda!" laughed Pang.

"**YOU** are a panda **TOO!**" laughed Ping.

Then, every day, Ping and Pang met
on a different side of Panda Palace,
and did their favorite thing...
together.

Conversation Starters for Parents & Educators

Q. How are Ping and Pang different from each other? How are they alike?

Q. Why do you think that at first, Pang and Ping don't get along? How do they become friends?
Talking points for parents/educators: tolerance and acceptance of other people's differences. Also, it can be scary stepping outside one's comfort zone.

- In the story, Ping says, "I'm Ping. I'm a panda!" And Pang replies, "No way!" Pang doesn't think Ping could also be a panda, because Ping seems so different.

  Q. How do you think Ping feels when Pang says, "No way!"

  Q. And how do you think Pang feels when Ping reacts the same way?

- Think of some other kids in your life — siblings, friends, classmates, kids with whom you play sports, ride the bus, and so on.

  Q. In what ways are they similar to you? In what ways are they different?

Q. What's the food you love most in the world? Now, what if you met someone whom you liked a lot, but who didn't like that food? Could you still be friends? Why or why not?

- "Inclusive" is a good word to know. It means to include — to bring in, to welcome. It's the opposite of shutting out, ignoring, or pushing other people away.

  Q. What are some ways that you can be inclusive toward others?
  Talking point for parents/educations: kindness, empathy, respect. The importance of listening and thinking before you speak. Just because something is different doesn't mean it's "weird" or bad.

Mary Jane Begin is a Senior Critic in the Illustration Department at the Rhode Island School of Design (RISD), where she has taught for 28 years and serves as the Internship and Professional Development Advisor. Her latest teaching venture includes online video courses on color, composition, character development and media and materials with LinkedInLearning.com and CreativeLive.com. She is an award-winning illustrator and author of picture books including *Little Mouse's Painting*, *A Mouse Told His Mother, The Sorcerer's Apprentice* and *Willow Buds*, stories inspired by *The Wind in the Willows*, a classic tale that she also illustrated. Seven of her titles have been translated in Chinese, including her latest picture books, *My Little Pony, Under the Sparking Sea* and *The Dragons on Dazzle Island* published by Little Brown in collaboration with Hasbro. One of her titles, *Willow Buds, The Tale of Toad and Badger*, won the prestigious Bing Xin Children's Literature Award in China.

www.maryjanebegin.com   mjbegin1   MaryJaneBegin.Art

CPSIA information can be obtained
at www.ICGtesting.com
Printed in the USA
BVHW021946210621
609242BV00002B/2